Belongs to Mrs. Hodge.

Belongs to Mrs. Hodge.

Belongs to Mrs. Hodge

A Day with No Math

WRITTEN BY
Marilyn Kaye

ILLUSTRATED BY
Tim Bowers

HBJ

Harcourt Brace Jovanovich, Inc.

Orlando   Austin   San Diego   Chicago   Dallas   New York

ISBN 0-15-301037-1

2 3 4 5 6 7 8 9 10   071   95   94   93

For my godson, Alexandre Van Houten-Anselme

M.K.

To Brynne, Megan, Allison and our newest "addition"
(due in October)

T.B.

Sam was watching television when he heard his mother's voice. "Sam, did you do all your homework?"

"Almost all," Sam replied. "Everything except my math."

"Then please go to your room and do it," his mother said.

Sam went to his room. He read a comic book. He played a game. He looked at his stamp collection. Then he yawned. He washed up and brushed his teeth.

"Goodnight, M.C.," he said to the toy lion sitting on the bookshelf over the desk. "It's time for bed." Sometimes, when no one else was around, Sam talked to M.C. Of course, being a toy, M.C. didn't talk back to him.

Crawling into bed, Sam thought about the math homework he hadn't done. "I don't care," he said. "I'm sick of math.

Who needs math anyway? I wish there was no such thing as math." He pulled up his covers and gazed across the room at M.C.

"Wouldn't that be great, M.C.? No more math. No numbers, no adding, no subtracting. . . ." He reached over and turned out the light.

As he was falling asleep, he thought he heard a voice. "Your wish is granted." That's crazy, he thought sleepily. I must be dreaming.

The next thing Sam knew, it was morning. He sat up and did what he always did when he first woke up. He looked at the clock. But something was different today.

The clock had no numbers.

Sam rubbed his eyes and looked again. The face of the clock was still blank. He got out of bed and looked at his calendar. There were no numbers on it, either. He opened a book. There were no numbers on the pages.

"What's going on here?" Sam wondered.

"You got your wish," a voice answered.

"Who said that?" Sam asked.

"I did," the voice replied.

Sam's mouth fell open. "M.C.! You're a toy! How can you be talking?"

"This is a dream," M.C. said. "Anything can happen in a dream!"

Sam shivered. It was crazy. But he wanted to jump for joy. "My wish has come true! There are no numbers anywhere. That means no more math!"

Grabbing M.C., he ran down to the kitchen. "Let's make something special for your breakfast," said his mother.

"Can we make muffins?" he asked.

"Sure, that's easy," his mother said. "All we have to do is follow the directions." They opened a cookbook and looked at the recipe.

"Flour, sugar, baking powder, salt, eggs, milk, and butter," they read. They gathered everything on the list.

"How much flour do you put in?" Sam asked.

Mother looked at the recipe. "I don't know. There are no numbers here." So they threw everything together and mixed it up. Then they put it in the oven.

While the muffins baked, Sam brushed his teeth, combed his hair, and dressed for school. Then he went back to the kitchen.

"Yuck!" Sam shouted. Gobs of gooey batter oozed out of the oven.

"We'll have to make something else for breakfast," his mother said.

"Sam, is there enough time before the school bus comes?" whispered M.C.

Sam looked at the clock on the kitchen wall. "I don't know."

Then he heard a familiar sound. He hurried to the window and looked out. "Oh, no!" he yelled. "There goes the bus!"

Carrying M.C., Sam ran all the way to school. Sam hoped
they wouldn't be late for science. The class had planted bean
sprouts, and they measured them every morning. When the
sprouts were five inches tall, they would plant them outside.

Out of breath and panting, he tore into his classroom. Then
he gasped. "What's going on here?"

Streams of long bean sprouts practically covered the room.
They went up to the ceiling and twisted around the desks.

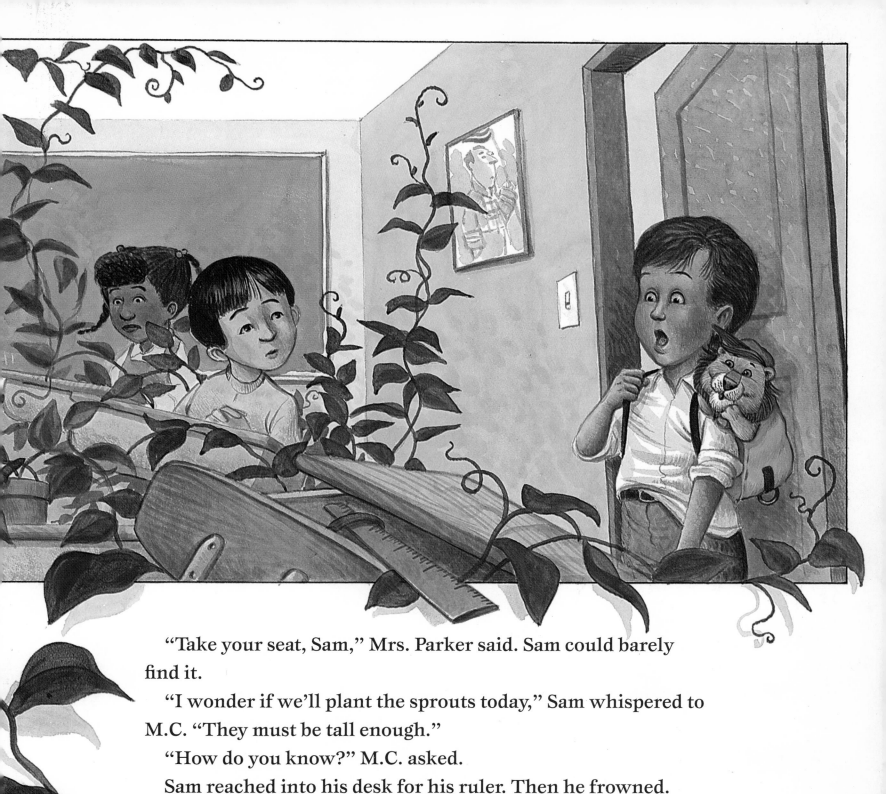

"Take your seat, Sam," Mrs. Parker said. Sam could barely find it.

"I wonder if we'll plant the sprouts today," Sam whispered to M.C. "They must be tall enough."

"How do you know?" M.C. asked.

Sam reached into his desk for his ruler. Then he frowned. The ruler didn't have any numbers. There was no way to know if the plants were five inches tall.

"We're going to have reading now," Mrs. Parker said. "Jana, would you and Sam please go to the closet and get the reading books?"

Jana and Sam went to the closet. They each gathered an armful

of books. "Do you think we have enough books?" Jana asked.

"I don't know," Sam said. "I guess so."

But they didn't get enough books. And sharing them wasn't very easy.

After they finished, Mrs. Parker said, "We can have art now."

Sam's stomach was growling. He raised his hand. "Is there enough time for art before lunch?"

"I don't know," Mrs. Parker said. "Now, class, would you like to draw or work with clay?"

"Let's use clay," Sarah called out.

"I want to draw," Joe said.

"Clay!" Sam yelled.

"Drawing!" Jana shouted.

Everyone was saying something different. "We should vote to make a decision," Mrs. Parker said. But no one could count the votes.

"I'm too hungry anyway," Joe said.

The whole class agreed. "Me, too!" "I'm starving!"

But when the class arrived at the cafeteria, they were so late that all the food was gone. There weren't even any apples left.

"This is terrible," Sarah complained. "I always eat an apple at lunch."

"Oh, well," Sam said. "It's time for recess, anyway."

When they went outside, Jana said, "Let's play kickball."

"I'll be captain of one team," Sarah announced. "Joe can be captain of the other team. We'll choose sides."

The teams gathered.

"Does this look right to you?" M.C. whispered to Sam.

Sam scratched his head.

"Not exactly. But I don't know what to do about it."

The game wasn't much fun. "What's the score?" Joe asked.

"Who knows?" Sam said. "There's no way to tell!"

By the time Mrs. Parker blew the whistle to end recess, they were bored with the game. And they didn't even know who won.

Finally, school was over for the day. "Do you want to go get a frozen yogurt?" Jana asked.

"Okay," Sam said. He needed something to cheer him up after a bad day. Joe and Sarah went with them.

"A blueberry frozen yogurt, please," Jana told the man at the counter.

"Chocolate for me," Sam said.

"I'll have strawberry," Sarah decided.

"Me, too," Joe said.

Sam placed his money on the counter.

"Is that enough money for a frozen yogurt?" M.C. whispered.

"I don't know," Sam said.

Jana, Joe, and Sarah couldn't add their money either. Neither could the man behind the counter. Nobody knew what to do! The frozen yogurt started to melt.

Hungry and sad, the kids left.

"What a terrible day," Sam said to M.C. when they returned home.

"Maybe that's because it was a day with no math," M.C. told him.

"That's silly," Sam said. "What difference does math make?"

"You really want to find out?" M.C. asked. "Let's wish for this day all over again. Only this time, put math back in."

That sounded like a silly idea to Sam. But it was worth a try. He closed his eyes and made the wish.

When he opened his eyes, it was morning again. Sam looked at the clock. He checked the calendar and the book. "All the numbers are back," Sam told M.C.

"That's going to make this day a whole lot better," M.C. said.

"I'm not so sure about that," Sam grumbled.

They went to the kitchen.

"Try making the muffins again," M.C. suggested to Sam.

Sam and his mother looked up the recipe in the cookbook.
"Let's see. Two cups of flour, two and one-half teaspoons of
baking powder, . . ." hummed Sam, as they mixed the ingredients
together. Then they checked the recipe again. "Bake at 400
degrees for twenty-five minutes."

"Better make sure there's enough time before the bus comes,"
whispered M.C.

    Sam looked at the clock. "It's 7:05 right now. That means the muffins will be ready at 7:30. The bus comes at 7:45. I'll have fifteen minutes to eat."

    While the muffins baked, Sam brushed his teeth, combed his hair, and dressed. By the time he finished, the muffins were ready, and Sam and his mother ate a delicious breakfast. Then he went outside to catch the bus.

When Sam arrived at school, he measured the sprouts. "Mrs. Parker," he said, "the bean sprouts are well over five inches tall."

"Good," Mrs. Parker said. "Let's plant the sprouts outside."

After they planted the sprouts, it was time for reading. Jana and Sam went to the closet and gathered books. "Do you have enough for everyone?" M.C. whispered.

"Let's see," Sam said. "There are twenty kids. Jana, how many books do you have?"

Jana counted the books. "There are seven here."

"I've got eight," Sam said. "That makes fifteen. We need five more."

When they finished reading, Mrs. Parker said, "We can have art now."

Joe raised his hand. "Do we have enough time for art before lunch?"

Mrs. Parker looked at the clock. "Oh, dear. We don't. It's already 11:45 and lunch is at noon! Thank you, Joe."

This time, the class made it to lunch on time, and Sarah got her apple.

When they returned to class, the students voted to pick an art project. They counted the votes. Fourteen students wanted to draw, and six wanted to work with clay. "It looks as if we'll draw today," Mrs. Parker said.

At recess, Sarah and Joe were team captains for kickball. They took turns choosing their teams, so they each ended up

with the same number of players. It was an exciting game.
M.C. kept score.

"Who won the game?" Mrs. Parker asked after she blew the
whistle.

"The score was five to five," M.C. whispered.

"It was a tie," answered Sam.

After school, Sam, Jana, Joe, and Sarah went to the frozen-yogurt store. "Do you each have enough money for a cone?" the man asked.

Sam counted. "I've got a quarter, two dimes, three nickels, and five pennies. That makes sixty-five cents."

"I've got seventy-five cents," Jana said. Joe and Sarah had sixty cents each.

"Look!" Sam said. "Super-Duper Special Frozen Yogurt Sundae! Five flavors! Three fruit toppings! Only two dollars!"

"But no one has two dollars," Sarah said.

"Yes, you do," M.C. whispered to Sam.

"If we add our money all together," Sam exclaimed, "we have two dollars and sixty cents. More than enough!"

"But that's enough for just one sundae," Jana said.

"Yeah," said Joe. "Let's get four spoons!"

The sundae was the best treat they ever had. It was huge! And they had enough money left over for pretzels to eat on the way home.

"That was great," Sam said to M.C. when they returned home. "What a terrific day." He lay back on his bed and closed his eyes. When he opened them, it was morning.

"I thought that day was too good to be true," Sam sighed. "It was just a dream, like the first day." He looked at the clock. It was 7:05. "I've got 40 minutes before the bus comes. It takes me five minutes to get dressed, and ten minutes to eat breakfast. I could lie here in bed for 25 minutes. Or . . . I could do my math homework."

Suddenly, that didn't seem like such an awful job anymore. He looked up at his toy lion. "That was a pretty strange dream, M.C. Who would ever guess that a day with no math could be such a terrible day?"

Of course, since this was real life, M.C. didn't answer. But as Sam looked at him, he noticed something around the lion's mouth.

No, Sam thought, it wasn't possible. This was just too weird. After all, it had been a dream, right?

But that stuff on M.C.'s face . . . it certainly *looked* like frozen yogurt.